Your library Sefto

Please return this item by the due date:

2 7 ... 2018

Please return this item by the due date
or renew at **www.sefton.gov.uk/libraries**
or by telephone at **any** Sefton library:

Bootle Library **0151 934 5781**
Crosby Library **0151 257 6400**
Formby Library **01704 874 177**
Meadows Library **0151 288 6727**
Netherton Library **0151 525 0607**
Southport Library **0151 934 2118**

your Library Sefton

Sefton Council

Frank the frog hops to the pond.
With a quick plop, he jumps in.

Frank kicks his legs.
He can swim well.
He swims to the pad
and gets up on to it.

Frank needs a rest, so he sits still
on the pad.
His leg is in the pond.

Just then, a big fish swims along.
It is looking for food.

Look out, Frank!
Lift that leg out of the pond!
The big fish will have you
for lunch.

Snap! The fish attacks.
But Frank is too quick.

He jumps on to the back
of the fish.
The fish bends its back.
Can it push Frank off?

Then Frank hops on to its fin.
The fish flicks its fin.
Flick!

So Frank skips on to its tail.
The fish flips its tail.
Flip! Flop!

Then Frank is back in the pond.
Quick, Frank! Swim!

Look out, Frank!
This fish has sharp teeth.
It will get you if you are not
quick.

The fish swims after Frank.
Will it have Frank for lunch?

No! Frank is in luck.
There is some green weed
in the pond.
The weed stops the fish.

Frank can swim into the weed,
but the fish cannot.
The weed is too thick.

Frank gets out of the pond.
With a hop, a skip and a jump,
he gets away.
Good job, Frank!